P9-DUB-565

KISS THE SKIN OFF

CHERRY VALLEY EDITIONS

1985

Lyn Lifshin

Skin Off

Cover: STAR welded steel sculpture by Dion Wright, 1974,
photograph by Robert Torrez

Some of these poems have appeared in the following magazines: Wormwood, Thunder Mountain, Ms., Sojourner, Clock Radio, Jump River Review, 13th Moon, Feminary, Poetry Now, Hawaii Review, Falcon, North American Review, Panhandler, Hampton Sydney Review, Lips, Chelsea, Massachusetts Review, Shirt Off Your Back, Pig in a Poke, Moosehead, Apple, The Little Magazine, Greenfield Review, Centennial Review, Another Chicago Magazine, Granite, Calyx, Stooge, Kayak, Poetry Now, Beloit Poetry Journal, Naked Charm, Epoch, New Letters, Bellevue Press, Bellingham Review, Hanging Loose, The Smith, Rhino, Rolling Stone, and American Poetry Review.

Special thanks to Richard Aaron, Am Here Books, Santa Barbara, CA.

Library of Congress Cataloging in Publication

Lifshin, Lyn.
  Kiss the skin off.

  I. Title.
PS3562.I4537K5   1985   811'.54   84-17035
ISBN 0-916156-69-9
ISBN 0-916156-70-2 (pbk.)

Cherry Valley Editions are distributed by:

Beach & Company, Publishers
3510 Olympic Street,
Silver Spring, MD 20906

Thanks to
  Yaddo, Millay Colony, & MacDowell Colony
  where some of these poems were written

PREFACE

I am pleased to select these poems of Lyn Lifshin's for this award-winning book.

She, among many, knows what a struggle it is to be heard in today's multitude of poets. It would be difficult for me to think of a due she hasn't paid; a praise she hasn't earned.

It is comforting to know that there is such a voice in my generation strong enough to defy the efforts of so many who'd rather keep it muffled while pushing other voices of other players of other games. But, like great poetry of the past, her work continues to rise, and it becomes more and more apparent that it will easily find its place in American literature among Stein, Dickinson, Bishop, Plath, and Sexton no matter what clucking and consternation it produces from those who try to force poetry into their own cubicles, to try to make it fit their own confines and order, starting at the throat of the "status quo" and working up.

We know that any great poetry of America has always upset the status quo and in this case may well lay it out from head to toe.

Charles Plymell
Washington, DC
October 29, 1984

KISS THE SKIN OFF

FROM A WOMAN GONE MAD

tell them that the
blue under my
wrists has backed
up into my head
like a sewer
clotted with leaves

SUN POEM

honeysuckle
bees my
skin smells
of sun the
insides of
roses. I want
to eat that
light. Every
thing that
grows does

I SPENT MY FIRST MARRIAGE AT THE MOVIES

which, in its own
way was as unique
as the movies we
selected: Late
August at the Hotel
Ozone, the Virgin
President we
didn't want what
everyone else was
supposed to be

starved for like
Doris Day movies.
What we got was
not what we
wanted. In the
glow of the screen,
more flattering
than moonlight,
for a long time
tho we dreamed
we could

THE STRANGE TOWARD MORNING DREAM

after talking how
distracting it is having
colonists in each other's
beds having the last
week sucked up pretty
soon we'll be leaving
a man who looks like
my father when he
was 18 suddenly is
rubbing my back there's
a couch and a too long
reading I put my head
on his lap want his
hand on my hair notice
his penis thickening we're
half asleep when there's
a banging at the door
it's his wife he never told
me she was deformed
ugly flippers a beak
and claws lashing at my
chenille bathrobe asking
if I gave readings in it

IRRITATION

starts off small
8 fur balls of sweet
fur you can
hold in your palm
so small if they
peed you
wouldn't notice
you go out for

a few days
suddenly there's
8 large snarling
tom cats pissing
in corners
tearing the couch
It's may or june
before you open
the apartment door on
the 4 family unit
where all the
windows are
wide open you
are knocked down

PAVAROTTI AND MEHTA ON TV

under the electric blanket
and quilts with the
shutters closed against
the moon's icy fingers
the cat curled into
himself like a fist a
comma separating things
from each other like the
spaces this week. I

understand the Japanese
woman writing a suicide
goodbye to her one
friend, an old tv
The wine should be
better warm and full of
spices, tonight
should be too. Then I
feel the music take
me like a lover I
didn't think could
reach pull me out of
where I was in a
cage of ice feel the
ice turn to water
all over me

LANIA

which isnt her real name
in a pink satin blouse
like mine has stolen my
long skirts large brown
eyes pieces of poems that
leave huge chunks twitching
in a snowdrift calling
for you to pull them,
they want to be brought
back to a room with a
sloped ceiling hung with
quilts and a woodstove
Lania is those left out
pieces burns like pine
with a good updraft
so thin she could have
come out of Auschwitz tho
she sees herself after a

meal too fat to pose
naked She has on long
dangling earrings velvet
pants that bag more than
they should blood red
near the ankles where they
are wet with snow in a
studio that seems familiar
where she'll write two
lines with a blurred type
writer ribbon late and
having to run. She burns
fast but not well leaves
something sticky

ON RAPPLE DRIVE

after supper women
calling the children
back from the sand

thru tumbleweed
their faces stained
with berries

Kathy Jimmy
Tommy a boat

rocking in leaves

Lonnie the sing
song second syllable
shipwrecking a
little Davey

Mary Nancy
like a child
calling a lost
cat home in
the night

some say its the
last thing men
dying in fire
in explosions hear

SNOW WHITE
for years locked in a
development of ranches
forgetting how to drive
she went to bed and
rose up as a virgin
got all A's
passed her Italian
thighs pale soft as snow
not that anybody would
notice on Rapple
Roar of power motors like beasts
tumbleweed blown from the
mountains like the dream
she walks into suddenly
in rooms full of strange
stooped little men
all anxious to prove their
virility as shorter
men often do. She didn't
have anything else to
do and always had done
what was expected was
always anxious to please so
she let them see them

18

selves in her the way
they wanted tall and as
straight as a live oak
she cleaned the carpets
with ivory snow dreaming of
lost teeth, witches
ordering clothes from FBS
ordering books from a
catalogue so no evil
could slip in disguised as
an encyclopedia salesman
or a republican candidate
for city hall until having
a weakness for apples she
bites in deep falls in
to a blue daze is someone
in a bell jar until she
spits out what she swallowed,
rescues herself

MAMMOGRAM

wild birds in me
clot under the
eaves Monday I'm
wrapped in white like
a bride or corpse
someone says when I walk
by there's a smell
of roses I feel snow
stain my cheeks some
thing in me flecks away
like wood left all
winter under a frozen
pond what's there

makes patterns I
don't recognize lost
bottles in whirlwinds
with messages I am
desperate to read

RAVEN

in velour the color of fur
that would glow at midnight
her sheets smell of musk
dried leaves and apples
Birds slam thru the halls.
Nothing is done in moderation.
The ceiling the color of sun
in the desert at noon.
Patchouli puts its lips on you
Nothing here is pale or
light or fades into something
else like sand colored rugs.
With a name like Raven of
course her hair is midnight.
wild and sleek and smells of
damp leaves wind. Coals
glow her eyes glow her skin
when she lies on the sofa
and kicks off her shoes.
Walls pull away from the
ceiling. Nights steam,
are rich as lasagna.
Jangling comes from
rusty pipes 7 o'clock
bubbling with garlic and
parmesan cheese. Wine glows

in oversize glasses
like rubies. She is always
starved burns like the
cigarettes she lights
one after another.
The names of her birds
translated from Swahili
are I want everything
and more

CAP COD, 1983

20 years ago I sat
in the backseat of
the Caddy let clam
wind curl my hair
I was dreaming of
being skinny
counting
which men whistled
dreamed in my white
old fashioned dress
with a plum velvet
belt of being loved
or of being famous
It doesn't seem so
long ago In twenty
more years I'll be
an old lady maybe
sit near the dunes
in a quilt of gulls
smell pines in wind
that's damp as skin,
hug the same moon

1959

Elvis was hot
even in Middlebury
where I jitterbugged
with a boy from
Birmingham

you could hear
Otter Creek from the
apartment where
Louise and I began
wondering about
our breasts we

were bored not
popular we didn't
want to sit and watch
the big Zenith tv

while cheerleaders
like Joyce Menard
went across the
state line we
wanted to buy a
Greyhound ticket
west for 30
dollars where you
could hear Wolf
Man Jack when
there's a full moon
in Seattle

ELVIS

dead in the house
as sun glittered on
a string of Cadillacs
chrome like neon
derringer in his
book on stage
in a drawer
diamonds

60 year old women
in Nevada 12 year
olds in Texas
cry people

cry in the streets
I don't believe
they say ask if
it's a mistake

GRACELAND CEMETERY

drivers on cold rainy
nights especially in
september with leaves
streaked across the
creosote see a woman
wrapped in satin
white in the gates
to the graveyard they
offer her a ride she
gets in but when they
get down to lark st
there's just a pool

of water a sleepy
woman at the door
who says it's nothing
it's my daughter it
happens in the rain
she seems to want
to come back here
you understand of
course that she's
been buried up there
for nearly 4 years

MEMPHIS AUGUST 17 1977

sky the color of cocaine
mourners line up near Graceland
just the image of gold on gold
strutting swiveling swaggering
now or never
all shook up
loving you

OLD MEN HOTEL BRENNER

they are like plants
put out on the porch
that only bloom at

night when the light
won't burn those
leaves that dissolve

by morning. Chairs
and teeth click.
Smells of garlic
roses the word

yesterday like a
pile of bones a
necklace of stories
they thread with
their own hair
from these strings
they make a

harp to play
in the snow as
the holidays
blur. Those who

don't come back
next August are
added become
strings for the
fingers left
to touch

YOU DON'T ENUNCIATE HE SAID I CAN'T READ YOUR LIPS

he said his father
used to take them out
on Sunday tell them to
make each syllable so
clear nothing ran to
gether but your words
are like leaves in
a storm soaked to
gether so you can't pick
one up without the
other or blown so fast
birds couldn't catch
up. We're eating
hamburgers in booths

a little too bright
my mouth fills with
feathers the birds in
me wanting to fly
wanting to weave
pieces of colorful
threads and branches
into a nest warm as
thighs tangling around
mine where no lips
need to be looked at
to be read

INSOMNIA LIKE ANTS

worse on a night
it's hot and sticky
you can almost hear
it climbing the
walls in your
head ready to
plop on you
you curl in a
ball of yourself
as if to shut
off any opening
but it finds
a way in crawls
over your eye
lids just as
sleep begins
sucking you in

ATLANTIC CITY

I've taken too many
clothes with me
lugging them with
locks exploding
breaking packing
and unpacking in
different rooms
with my mother say
ing yes or no like
she will too
long when it comes
to men this is
before i kick the
person i hate most
on paper when i
still fight with
whoever i'm with
and then put on the
green and blue
dress that's like
a sarong and makes
me feel exotic
i feel the space
between me and the
cloth skinny at
107 and then walk
6 hours on the board
walk teasing with
my hips and eyes
tho my mother will
never let me high
anyway on what
i have gotten
rid of the one
part of me i knew
i was better off
without

BLUE PIECES OF CHINA, SLIVER OF SPOON

sharp as the
words they spit
at each other,
leaving with as
little trace as
indians when the
rain forsakes them
Only what's broken
and pieced like
words on tape
just before the
pilot crashes
can be pieced to
gether like
words eavesdropped.
Flowers grow over
where they were
as if it was
a battlefield
or a grave

THE OLD HUNCHBACK IN THE CHICKEN HOUSE

out here I got lots
the things I brought back each
trip to the dump broken
bicycles pieces of a radio
you see this Ronson I

just brought back and put
a bolt on the bottom good
as new and this Frigidaire
almost makes ice cubes
see this pack of liver

wurst I didn't eat meat
much before I had that field
of apples. Oh I do feel glad
you came let me show you
how I sealed the wind out
and the dolls I found in
the ashes. The Last Supper
over his bed scissors a
Coca Cola girl cut out
and tacked to the door

I never married
this time of year the
apples start I pulled the
sumac and nettles from
that whole hill every

thing I need is in this room
you got to look where you
wouldn't expect it's
easy for me bent over as
I am I don't miss much

WHEN I HEARD HIM SAY

she expected him to
perform the word was
like those dark metal
hooks you see strapped
into a dentist's chair
elbow with a sharpened
point and I was think
ing if I could just
pad myself with enough
men they'd be a moat
bandage to keep from
feeling what was
jabbing me

I DIDN'T WANT TO

kill that mouse
but the way he
was making a nest
in me scooping
out holes in the
night and filling
it with loud
scratches and
pieces of string
if he'd gone a
bout things quiet
ly I'd have been
able to let him
live behind the
desk might even
have grown to like
knowing of his
presence but he
was arrogant left
pieces of himself
to flaunt the
territory he'd
taken. Love, like
that, I didn't
want to spring
something so final
on you. Would it
be better for
both of us to be
dragging our traps
in wild pain

SUNDAY

the fresh wood
attracts bees
they blow in from
the blood maples
head toward the
sweet sap. All
afternoon,
the sound of men
laughing clomp
of the wood be
ing halved or
quartered opened
up soaking up the
hot sun the men
sweat and roll
up their sleeves
the sun is coming
into the wood
seasoning the
hard oak now
it's time for
the apple wood
In my room the
sweet smell of
clover water
underground sun
thru my black
wool sweater.
I could be that
wood you
could burn

REMEMBER THE LADIES

women who wouldn't
till they married

but the house was so
cold snow blowing
in thru the daubing
like the cry of starving
wolves and branches

knocking oiled paper
like hands crawled

under the covers
in their clothes
kept a board be
tween them thought

of a thigh maybe
warm skin flung
over the sheets
smelling of skin
and hair next

morning pulled on
wool and heavy leather

before lugging water
out for the cows
breath steaming life
fog in the willows

JEANNE MARIE PLOUFFE

small and dark behind
your mother's full
skirts, cleaning
other people's houses.
Florence and I imagined
worms slithering thru you
when you ate lumps
of sugar in my grand

mother's bathroom,
still stayed thin.
Eyes like cloves
under huge lashes in

classes you wouldn't
say a word in. "Canuck"
the boys called out
over Otter Creek

Bridge as your legs
got less spindly and
the girls from college
professors' homes

didn't invite you.
People said your last
name with the tone
they'd say tramp.

Your skin creamy,
your hair curled with
night. There wasn't
a boy who didn't

think he could put
his hand inside
your dress. You
never said anything,

as if part of you
was already gone,
as if there was
some place to

go to. Once, singing
of Quebec, your eyes
gleamed like the
gold cross boys yanked

from your neck and tossed in
the snow. I heard
the trailer burned
down, the survivors

headed north. Jeanne
Marie if you read
this please
write me

IN THE DREAM

My mother says look,
I'll show you why I
can't go to the party
tonight, takes off
her blouse, back
toward me. I see no
thing, a dime sized
bump I never would
have noticed with a

cut across it. My
mother, who never
complained, cooked
venison when the
hurricane blew a
roof off the
Steinberg's house and 13
people slept in our
beds the day some
thing was cut out of
her, blood still
dripping. My mother
who could open jars
no one else could,
who never stayed in
bed one day, says
the small circle
hurts, I press her
close, terrified
I'm losing what
I don't know.

THE PEARLS

an engagement present,
from my husband's parents.
Shoved in a drawer
like small eggs
waiting to hatch for
gotten they seemed
like something in a
high school photograph.
I'd have preferred
a large wrought iron
pendant beads that
caught the sun.
Pearls were for them

and I was always
only a visitor
tho he said he
wished I'd call him
Dad. Sam was all I
could get out
it was hard to
throw my arms a
round to bubble and
kiss and not just
because they thought
me a hippie a witch,
took their son's
car and stamps and
coin collection.
Pearls wouldn't go
with my corduroy
smocks long black
ironed hair. They didn't
blend with my hoops
of onyx and abalone
that made holes in
my ears but caught the
light. Pearls might
have gone with the
suits I threw away no
longer a graduate student
trying to please. They
weren't suitable for
days with a poet hidden
in trees or for throwing
up wine in toilet bowls
after poetry readings
where I shook and swore
not to let anyone see.
My spider medallion is in
at least 8 poems. Pearls

remind me of the way I
thought I was: studious
but not wild not interesting.
But I put those pearls
on last night tho I
hadn't planned to wear
them they didn't seem
ugly or apt to choke,
seemed gentle and mild
as so little in my life
is these days. I
slept in nothing but
those pearls they
seemed part of me

GETTING THE GOODS

In recent months, according to reports from Thailand
published in the Far Eastern Economic Review, murdered
infants have been used to transport heroin across the
border from Thailand to Malaysia

A wind blowing thru
dark elephant grass
a blood sun over the
rice fields a man

holds an infant underwater,
black hair snakes the
child gurgles then
doesn't a plastic rattle

bobs on the water like a
head before the water goes
from blood to wet bark
the child is slit

emptied out like a trout
or a hen stuffed taut
and plump with small
bags of heroin

and before the moon is
a pale grape in the
musky night a woman paid
as well as the dead

child's mother will wrap
the corpse in a shawl
hug it close seeming to
smoothe the damp

hair into place as if
snuggling a sleeping
baby getting the
goods over the border

ALBERTA HUNTER

long gold hoops flashing
eyes flashing hands
on her hips nothing
on her isn't moving
"gonna lay it on
you" born in
Memphis got a
nickel for bread
went to Chicago
"never knew my kisses
meant so much never
dreamed life had so"
85 laying it on
you dancing
belting it

hair pulled
straight back not
to miss anything

RUE DU FEU

I wake from a dream
of my father and think
of the man I held
more tightly in
shadows of Notre Dame.
When I wrote notes
for this I could
remember the smell
of his hair how I
touched his wrist to
see the time later
wrote: "that tattoo
I wouldn't see again"
I don't remember
the design even
why I let him
press me up against
grey stones in the
alley I was a
bird that had slid
thru bars something
on a chain feeling a
link break sun so
hot. September. my
suede short skirt
shorter if I leaned
over to tie my boots.
"live with my sister
you won't need paper."
I took his cigarette
tho I never smoke.
I would have taken
anything

REMEMBER THE LADIES

obstetric case with
tools of wood brass
and leather steel

and wool midwives
walked thru the
acorns pushing
on sleds thru the
snow as the wind
was howling

snow blowing thru
oil cloth in windows

a woman rolling her
head in down pillows
trying to believe in
4 months she'll be
gathering violets

a daughter in a basket
near the bed sees the
forceps covered with
gauze and greased with
hogs lard this huge dark
metal seems too big
to go between any legs

MY MOTHER'S KNIFE

tonight she calls she
remembers when it must
have happened the year
you know she says when
the trees slammed down

That was when I started
missing remember they
came because their
roof had blown away
It would have been
easy enough to take
something bigger
all the people and no
lights I've looked 19
years and couldn't find
a knife like that it
makes me boil when I
saw it in her kitchen
I should have said
Sally that's mine but
she was saying how she
needed couldn't get
along without that
knife wherever it
came from. My mother
stops in Macy's knife
department each time
she comes mourns the
gone steel the perfect
dark brown handle
She dreams this knife
is why Sally's a
little cool and doesn't
want anyone to just
drop by

SOMEWHERE IN THE MIDWEST

a man can almost hear
the wind cracking
frozen cornstalks
When he lets the cat

in cold glows around
the silver fur like
those rings around the
moon that mean some
thing's happening.
He hums a blues tune
in a cold room full
of paper. This could
be Madison or may
be Red Granite he
could remember a
woman he held one
night with hair
longer and blacker
than it was. If
he decides she's just
a travelling lady
he puts down the
phone listens
to branches doesn't
write what he feels
in a room
as cold as hers
where she hears
the frost etching
the moon out too

MIDWEST

all that sky
a flat black
with only a cat's
eyes blazing

people wait alone
wind changes in
the cornleaves
people hear it like

a chord augmented.
Houses chip slowly
stranded in snow
Only the sky is fast

NEARING SEVENTY SHE HAS

trouble opening jars
but wants to learn to
disco. I never wanted
to dance so much as
I do lately she says
in a dress slit to
the waist that I had
when I was 20. Salt
and peppery hair to
her shoulders eyes
bubbly fudge or a
deer's that broke
thru a tangle of
cars to reach the
tall thin apple trees
squeezing thru con
crete near the apart
ment window,
decided to move inside
and stay. My mother
fills the room with
summer in New York
City the glass of
bourbon she downed on
a dare as Ruthie

and Frieda tried to
shove her into a
cold shower and
the man whose glasses
broke when she
pushed him away and
he said you've made
an ass of me and she
said I didn't have
to do that fill
the front room on
Main Street where
she still dances to
Cab Calloway I can
smell the damp shawls
on the night boat
to Staten Island see
the blue and white
long silk skirt
flare and swirl

LIPS IN THIS HOUSE

some are parched
longing for water
for any place wet
For them September
is the Cocohuilla
Desert parts
of them flake away,
leave what's left
more sore and
longing

the lips of the ice
madonna would freeze
dry your nights if

they brushed your
fingers gangrene
blooming where she
presses them together
so hard her teeth
seem to curve in the
better to bite any warmth
she might almost swallow

her lips are perfect
as her legs,
as unwilling to open
there are the lips
that never close
sucking on scotch
and creamed bread
pudding sucking
whatever comes her
way left over
chicken a man
who can't eat fat
except for hers

her teeth are white and
glow when she
brays as she's
coming shaking the
glass in the house break
ing windows she licks
everybody's platters
clean

under the hemlock
the oldest lips in
the house savour crumbs
storing up for a
long winter saving what there

is, knowing it will be
gone as the memory of
his wife's laughing
her black and purples
her silks

some lips taste like
chartreuse lose them
selves in the green
of that would
lick the pines
for that color

In the room of mahogany
and cherry lips press
the marble bust
instead of a lover

the composer's lips
suck his hand
not able to
reach lower
they try to suck
on her ear slurp
up the ringing
like the soft yellow
poached egg

lips full as thighs
lips that juicy
lips that bite on
themselves like
guilt

lips moving on skin
instead of fingers
lips instead of words

lips that lie as
easily as words
lips that leave a mark
where they've been
careless lips lips
that keep secrets
lips that can only whisper
lips that can just pout

the lips down there
the lips opening under
the dark black carved table
round as someone calling
for help in the night
silent as the lips of
stone in the garden
filling with icicles
melting again

there are the poet's lips
that would suck a
tongue a penis
chewing an ear of
corn butter drips from
her chin and fingers

the novelist runs
her tongue over hers
as if it were
someone else's

some are scarred by
words spit out leaving
with such a
hiss they
couldn't come home

some are painted
almost a mask
almost a personna

some are stained with smoke
one smells like pernod

there are lips that quiver
thinking of a husband's
death 12 years after
the words fall out
like flesh from bones
of skeletons in a
coffin with soft shudders
the other lips hold on
to themselves
or press a wine glass,
swallow

some lips are packing
leave with more
than they came with

there are the quiet lips
you see open like a
flower lips like
bowls you could drink from
lips like a tub
lips like a toilet
lips that don't open
till they're asleep
the ones flecked with blood

lips that try to reach
up and hold their
nose as the
beaver skulls boil

lips that try to eat the
black paint wedding cake
lips that will try anything
lips that run back to the room

some stay up all night
walk in the trees
before breakfast
some are glued to other lips
imagining it doesn't
show some are longing
for other lips
imagining it doesn't
show some whistle a

tune from a Chinese
grandmother some
are ringed with hair
some want to be glued
inside rings of hair
that won't ever cool
some lips are so hot
even the coolest mineral
water even baths laced with
lithium don't cool them
they stay awake all night
moaning like doves are
like one half of a lip
that's lost the other

WILD HORSES DYING WHERE THE LAND BECOMES A DESERT

after the fourth day
they stood and swayed
like a weight on
a rope that
moves when nothing
seems to move it
they fall against
each other
crumbling stones
brick turning to dust
the horses are dying
of dust pneumonia

they are so light
the wind moves them
they could be water

hooves and hair
in the rippled sand
like shells

ANOTHER EASTER

he said madness was growing
in his mother's chest
and it spread its
stain on him

but in the trees the green
came early it grew a
cross the windows ice
slid from us

and nothing flooded
it happened so fast overnight
trillium and columbine
white styrofoam

floated in the sun on the
blue pond that other
years still had been
frozen and it was

whatever anyone
in the sun, shoulders
touching, could have wanted
it to have seemed

UNDER THE HOUSE

a fencing helmet stuck
between the beams
flower pots stuck
way off in the dark
earth floor no one
quite finished mice
doze in the corners
the wires twist like
veins and arteries
to a heart some
where ashes slip
thru a chute pieces
of some dream or fear
building up under
the house

JACKSON AVE

painting windows gold
for a reason i don't
remember a virgin
after 10 months of
marriage the cats
were the only things
growing i stuffed
them in the closet when
the landlord came to
cut down the lilacs
there was never
mail on wednesday
we went to his
mother's and i pretended
to care about soap
flakes and never
exploded when she'd
pull out a can of
baby gerber's say if
you really loved
us if you weren't
like a crazy woman
with those cats you'd
be getting ready
to need this

THE ORIGIN OF HOT AND COLD
ACCORDING TO THE DELAWARES

a man and a woman
started fighting
they lived, it was
far north and cold,
so she went into
the hotlands. But

he got lonely, rode
south and brought
the cold. Wherever
he went it was
winter. They did
this every year

LOSING CONNECTION

i'm in a hurry running back to the
house to pick up clothes
3 weeks dissolve

i'm tearing thru rooms velvet
pants flesh jersey beads
i'm with my mother

sometimes i'm
not and go to a
liquor store with a fat

man i hate. i
forget why i'm doing
this i'm losing

things to connect
with what went
before and go to call
someone i'm
already forgetting
frost on the telephone booth

glass i can't find a
Everything in my pocket book
spills people waiting

in line growl look
there's just quarters i'm
sweaty feel fat tho i

just weigh a 100. The
number bleeds in my hand
thru the glass the mouths get
wider. If i can just walk thru
these people if these men
will leave me

even the butcher winks at
me someone is saying
sexy When i peel

the hands off
faces blur look im a
poet i scream smelling
my skin it's words
that i and the telephone
screams back yr 3

minutes are That last
metal and plastic kiss and
then the door jams

THE FEAR BEE

gets in yr sheets
buzzes where you
can't somehow its
like losing a
needle a jackknife
in the deep brown
chair Sunday you're

seven reading the
funnies gramp turns
The Shadow down in
the den closes
the door you go
to sleep hearing
grownups laugh
slap cards you're
deep in the warm
brown ok with
everybody but the
needle could be a
bee close to you
stinging you at
night when arms
that carried you
from the furry
chair to the car
to tuck you in
cold sheets
close the door

THE EAST IS UNDER A DARK CLOUD

the mad girl is pacing
in her room her head
full of the darkest
weather there's

a hurricane under
her skin that old
going in different
directions blues
she can't read her
own lines on the page
the wind is increasing
it's freakishly cold

for this time of year
someone in ohio
is uncertain the
new york lover
knows somethings
threatening feels
the shutters rattling
down his backbone

MARYA

with her leaves in the
tritons with her
ghosts and yellow
scarves she
leaves the door with
a chalk mark and
feels it open
feels her death
feels the woman who
died in nineteen
fifty in the lilac
wind this june
she is under 30
she was plain
polly smith
from topeka she
would have taught
violin and never
run thru the trees
in velvet waited in
drab hotel lobbies
knocked into by
dopers whores

and known she was go
ing to die soon
and suddenly had a
french accent and
a french name

SAWS

strange about people
buying saws especially
those who don't
need one the cool
novelist is saying
how he bought
one for woodstock
so i tell them about
my friend who
stole (along with
mismatched socks and
wine from porches) one
the august he lived
in the leaves while he
thought of dying
and that it must be
rusting under the ferns
and milkweed still. he
lit matches and i
fed him lasagne in
coffee tins so the
cats wouldn't get it
first. he never used
the saw, he never
planned to tho he
really wanted one.
saws must be and i
look around the table

my dress is too
shiny its my first
time in the house
and im scared but the
story is so peculiar
no one notices

TOO MANY READINGS TOO MANY MEN

performing is like
becoming wet after 17
orgasms in one
afternoon with nearly
half that many men
you're out of breath
from the showers
pulling on clean
nylon see thru
black bikini v's
so they can imagine
you in the way
they want to and
you smile and
say what you've
said for the 100th
time in a way that's
freshly deceptive
drawing them in
like a glistening
pink slit not letting
them see what was
once there isn't
as they drown in
what is in
their heads

BOOKS I BROUGHT TO THE LAST POETRY READINGS

there is the idea of them
on a table geraniums that
transform a muddy yard
or tombstones wrapping
what's what up in a
packaged form slivers
of wednesday boxed
and framed like fruit
that can never rot in a
drawing. It's almost as
if it was some replica
of you audiences will
lust to bring home like
Kennedy's face on a half
dollar this time will
be different from all the
rest you tell yourself
as if the book selling
was some new love and
you're hoping. Sure,
against odds, this time
no one gets ripped off,
stained bruised spines
broken covers but
just what each wants

EDITING THE ANTHOLOGY

wives of famous poets
send me their husbands'
pubic hair like thread
in a sampler that writes
out pick me

the poems lie
flat in a closet
like those black
bugs under a
log but
I know they're
waiting in the
dark, squirming
ready

upstairs even
isn't safe that
hum in the dark
special delivery
mosquitoes starved
for blood slipping
thru screens

if there's the
smallest opening
a swarm hatches
and they itch all night

I SHOULD HAVE KNOWN WHEN HE ATE THE ONE PROVOLONE SANDWICH

and then later shoved one slab
of his mother's cold pizza
into his face never saying he
was sorry there wasn't any
for me or when he stole the
jug of chablis at the poetry
reading along with massive
slabs of gouda and brie
oozing flattened under a
jacket somebody left by
mistake in his house that

this meant something like the
circle around the moon should
have seen signs of what would
come in the chamomile tea bag
dunked 25 times. Not that he
was Robin Hood if he brought
stolen wine to a party he'd
refill it and lug the bottle
back when it was time to go,
sulked if no one gave him books
or tickets or meat. Magazines
I hadn't even noticed were
missing little pieces of
string stamps he wove into
the nest it gave him cramps
to think the last woman had
run out on him leaving him
with the rent. He slugged
one man in the Texaco station
insisting he didn't owe an
extra seven cents because he'd
put in lead free by mistake.
In spite of skinny legs
and asthmatic ways people he
visited were often ready to
call the police. I should
have known after he ate
four meals without offering
anything to anybody. He thought
he could steal my heart as he
had gulped down the yogurt
slurping it down before he left
the store saving the cartons
Because he loved me so he
called me selfish pushy Jew
and broke into my bedroom
bit the wires then tried to

steal the cat and feed it
stolen mice and glassy wires.
He had as much going for him
as the tickets he threw a
cross the bed when he broke
the door whining I JUST wanted
to take you to this Buffy St.
Marie concert. In the tangle
of torn phones bruises ripped
cotton a few days later:
those tickets rose like
an oil slick stamped
with some singer's name I
never heard of, good only
for

February 1968

DOCTOR DOOMED

He wasn't the first man to
hate that poem or react like
a man to it the journalist
who wrote violent dirty
books said if you were my
wife and wrote anything like
it I wouldn't let you out
of the house. The man
she once was the wife of
said running out for the
last time "at least I won't
have to hear that poem
ever again." But during
the dinner before the read
ing she'd been subdued, knew
people would watch to see

how much she was drinking
and she kept her dignity
even with the professor's
hand up her thigh under the
table. The lasagne was
cooling too fast. This
doctor had been brought
because he'd said to some
one who was married aren't
you lucky. This doctor
had a goose and didn't
look like a midget Groucho
Marx as he'd been described.
He talked about wine and
eating out and tho he
talked a lot about which places
in Montreal and Burlington were
the most fun places at least
he talked and he only talked
about bladders and backs and
bones a couple of times. He
seemed to laugh tho perhaps
it was the lasagne catching
in the back of his teeth.
He seemed civil if not
interested she thought
feeling once the reading
was done she could relax
even tho her tight pants
were digging in. The night
was a glow except for the
way this doctor walked out
as she read "he poured
chocolate in my cunt." Others
seemed to think the poem
delicious. There was a real

cold wind when he left. Later
her sister said some people
like their chocolate in a cup

HE SAID HE SAW MY PICTURE IN ROLLING STONE

when he called he said he
wanted to explain the
situation that he was
a cross between Jagger
and a thin Max Von Sydow

he said he had to tell me
he was a famous a rock
star till it bored him he
wanted me to send him
photographs forget

the poems 3 or 4 perfect
nudes he said if he liked
them as much as my face
asked first did I have
flabby skin a 90 year old

body ass like the girl he got
from what porno mag he
wanted to make sure I'd
never had a baby my age
then he'd send me an

airline ticket and
maybe we could. It was my
face he said got to him Jane
Fonda's skin's too
oily he said he didn't

like bodies that drooped
or brown eyes since his
mother gave him away
he knew he could do
anything beat up
some famous poet

Poetry's too easy
he said he was light
but dark on the
inside asked me to read
a sexy poem and would
I mind if he came on
the phone imagining
my he was sorry it wasn't

a taller body. The girl from
the porno rag had
paid her own money to
meet him took off

her clothes in a bar
but she wouldn't do
Not much got to him
but my face looked
like one that would

was I a model he
asked did I know I
looked like Dylan's
ex wife had I
done it with women

in an airline wash
room with 4 in bed
Was I raped ever did
I have a hooked nose
was I jewish he wanted

to be sure truck
drivers turned when I
crossed the street
he went on finally
I guess his hand got
sticky I should have
but I couldn't hang
up

CO OP CITY READING

women with dyed apricot hair
say you're just like my
daughter rebelling and
she's in college too.

Love in the poems has risen
like a smoke ring on a
clear day and dissolved.
They never tasted that smoke.

I'd like a little book a
souvenir one woman in pale
blue mumbles and I begin
to feel like Plymouth Rock.

No one clapped for me as they
had for others' poems about
marriage, limoge and baby
daughters. My "Wild Women

Don't Get the Blues"
button blends with my dress
but not enough. A
man who couldn't hear

says he got what he could

out of it. Widows
eye me strangely their
red hair burns brighter

False teeth click. I
tell them that if they
thought the poems mean
they were black seeds

I must spit out, weeds
that would choke what
ever's growing. Cancer
is something I say

many think is caused
by anger that
didn't get out
blossoming, as if
that could help

ALL THE WOMEN POETS I LIKE DIDN'T HAVE THEIR FATHERS

I'm thanking you
Ben for letting me
be one too I
never could say
father and still
have trouble calling
anybody love. When
a man touches my
skin I just
think of bed (no
one has ever said I
wasn't sexy) Thank
you father (the one
place you are) and

for never letting
me know I was
pretty, for
making me need
paper to say
love. We
never talked and
last week I met
someone I wanted,
I couldn't let
him know.
Now I dream I
write him too and the
letters come back
stamped rejected.
There's not much
I trust. I know
you know what
that's like - with
your secret stock
market news scribbled
in books like poems
you couldn't show
anyone
looking at trees
alone too you
sat and watched
chestnuts drop
into the snow
Even with special
glasses my eyes
need prisms to
bend things.
Still I'm sorry I never
saw what you were,
what Russian pines
blew behind your

eyes that house of
chicken and goose
feathers dissolving
like the print of
your head finally
from the gold chair.
No one understood
why you would have
sliced us out of
your will wanting
your stocks to go on
like an eternal
flame some self
investing memorial
a space ship
knocked out of
orbit flashy
untouchable
as you were
except here where
I try to add the
pieces up like each
meal you paid for on
vacation in cape
cod in a small
notebook you kept
close to your
heart with those
pills. Like that
space ship there
was a place
neither of us
could reach that
still circles
and haunts

THE NIGHT SYLVIA PLATH DIED

Wind was whipping up Pennsylvania
Avenue, the tiger cat just a
kitten. Wind was sliding a woman
in a pea coat's hair out at
right angles. The hotel she'd
been bored waiting in had new tan
and brown carpet. Electricity
hissed like the tv set in

the storm that was coming, like
the eyes of her Greek stud. Wind
whipped her against the shoulders
of the man who would be with

her less time than the tiger
cat, the runt of the litter.
The man who had the fat brother
kitten, flattened on Crane Street,

plans a knot that will hang
from the door jamb and not
tear down the wood. In the
Japanese restaurant

knives gleam. It's Tuesday,
almost dark when a rat slivers
under the tables in the sleet
before any of the news

AFTER A DAY WE STAY IN BED TILL THE SUN IS CLOSE TO SETTING

he drives home
thru the black trees
with the poem a
bout me that will
make him famous
starting in his
fingers he wishes
the wheel were his
Olympia typewriter
he needs to get my
hair where he can
touch it on the long
drive thru the pine
trees my musk still
drenching the car
I want to read
this poem almost
as much dazed the
double night per
formance has sucked
me flat and pale
as an empty sheet
of nonerasable
bond has pulled

all color all the
wet moist verbs
out the way he took
the stories I told
and made them in
to his own surreal
dreams even my leaves
and branches
became the green
arms of a child

My mouth is dry I
need to have his
poem where my clove
nipples press into his
blue stripped cotton
smelling of sun
and wind in the pine
trees a mirror that
will reflect my dark
eyes I need this as
much as he needs to
invent me to
become himself

STUDENTS

they bring cheese and
wine curl like
stray kittens
at your feet,

a lover courting
you with things you
wouldn't expect.
This is the

first stage. They
are as appealing as
caterpillars no
one wants

around. You don't
need them. But
they need to nest
in your space.

Suddenly they've
weasled a way in
eaten all the leaves
and verbs in your
house stripped
your branches. Now
trees in your head are
dying. The students
fly away trans
formed butterflies
everyone is after

POETRY READING BENEFIT

There are ladies
in navy blue suits
who leave when some
one says prick in
a room where you
can hear it. It's
45 and there's only
cold apple juice.
The indian pulls
a blanket closer
There is a
long haired pale
thin woman in a
rose flowered
dress pulling
her arms so tight
around her you
nearly can hear
a rib crack. One
poet listens for
lines he can use and
jots them down on
a boot heel. None

of the poets have
a watch. The mike
hums and buzzes
and splats like a
nest of bees a
giant stamps on.
There is more pain
than apple juice.
The poet who talks
about splitting
wood and seeing his
breath over a
desolate frozen
stream has written
a thirty one part
poem about this.
Someone tries to listen
sniffing patchouli
as if that could
help. The poet
who is building
his body takes off
his clothes and
reads a poem
about how people
prefer wrestling
matches to poetry
readings and for the
first time so far
the audience knows
what he means

MURIEL RUKEYSER ACCEPTING AN HONORARY
DEGREE

with the night smelling of
rain that hasn't started.
Damp leaves a mist where
there will be roses. Muriel.
with her hair sleeked black
like someone trying never
to hide anything a figure
head on a ship hair blown
away from the sea wind.
The room is hot rustle
of programs. Black robes
black skirts and white
blouses. Bright red silk
rings beneath her robe
like a smile or a wave.
Her face uplifted near
the podium is that of
a woman looking up at a
lover, open feeling
sun warm on her skin
and the air all lilacs
who feels July stretch
ahead like route 107
in Kansas knows this
minute is everything

MARTHA GRAHAM

you have so little
time she says each
instant is so

exciting at
first in the early

days I was made
fun of I was
in my long

underwear I
took off my
bangles we
took women
off toe shoes
I wanted life
the way it
is

long neck her
lips like
a young girls
only dance if you
have to
if you
think you might
want a family
a home don't

her hair pulled
back her face
wide open

READING THOSE POEMS
BECAUSE I CAN'T GET
STARTED THINKING OF
THE PHONE CALL THAT
CAME, THAT YOU MIGHT

before i get to the
end of the line my
head's milkweed
something in me

drifts out into the
trees thru the
stained glass my
black seeds flying
out to where you
say we'll find
columbine they
get hung up in the
leaves words sinking
in where they can't
grow like what
was starting to
in the shot deer
left in the
snow all winter

ARTIST COLONY THE FIRST MORNING

when you hear
him snore and fart
thru thin partitions
when his toothbrush
drips down your
towel and the soap
disappears the
toilet seat is up
each time you
use it the smell
of spam and ham ooze
under his door and
coats your clothes.
I came here to
try to escape
something. un
grounded as the
moths that licked
my eyelids all night

His heavy footsteps
take over this poem,
black glass bead
eyes. We are
strangers stuck
facing each other
at breakfast lunch
at night sipping
wine, waiting
for someone else.
It's worse than
a marriage

ARMY BRAT

she should have known
after the first one
when they said she
had to leave school

leave the volley
ball team she never
kept the babies
in the house

like crazy sisters
people could smirk at
rolled them down
main street called

the first billy
they said she
must have thought
he would marry

finally even after
the second one she

saw him in dark
leafy rooms they'd

lean over the fire
escape above otter
creek walk
the babies down

frog alley then
she'd go down
Years of serving
her self up giving
so much away not
able to stop letting
him write his
name inside her

Or maybe she
just liked it
And the babies
who came like poems

that write them
selves in the
dark when you
hadn't planned them

FOR A MAN WHO LEAVES IN THE FALL WANTS YOUR FIRE BY DECEMBER

leaves with the wife
of a man who came
sunday to rent

the room he said
he was driving
north needed a
drink in another

city he won't
come home till
he's bored

or alone sick of
bars in saratoga
he says the women

are now dumb
chicks hates
sex a man like

this wants to keep
you crying he'll
pay the rent as

long as your eyes
are swollen shut
he never wanted
you to see much

when you start
walking he'll pour
ice on the stairs

drop in at 3 am
keep you up with
his talk of
dying he doesn't

want anyone else
to warm your bones

tho he'll never
do it he

never could
and he knows
hates your
singing your
poems will
tolerate you

sick phone you
drunk and say
he wants to

Listen

put a cactus in
your honey place
another in your

heart hang up
the phone

he'll go again
turn you into
a desert no
thing can live
in but tough
things that are
hard to touch

LOOKING THRU A PILE OF POSTCARDS

None of the
beauties are
smiling. Bacall
hid under a

hat nearly,
glances side
ways, lips half
a sneer. Harlow's
waiting as if
she knew for
what. Only
Gertrude Stein
doesn't look
like she's
squeezed into
a pose she can't
sit in, looking
straight ahead
50 maybe her
mouth open as if
she knew she
had some
thing to say

NAMES

lately i become
whatever you call
me the way some
indians do (i'd
been wanting to
trade or sell or
bury a lot of
what i am too)
For six days i
couldn't say ours
because it was
someone else's.
When you called me
love near the rag
shop on caroline

i tried to remember
the spell iroquois
put on names to
make them stay

THE LIBRARIAN

has given up women gets
only as close to them
as he can touch with
a feather. He wants
to make novels and poems
dreams his penis is a pen

that runs out of ink so easily
he edits his wife out of
the house, presses his
balls up against the dust of
dark card catalogues, burns to ram
the world with what's in his head

He wishes he was bigger, hides
behind an enormous desk. When
it comes to women he's
fast to revise. Any he can
lure into a dark space
he pounds and finds wanting

So he gives her the feather
stuffs her on an untouched
shelf, says she hasn't
any spine. He seals her lips
with library paste. If he
were to touch her breast it

would be with a memo saying
quiet this is not the
place to visit or talk. He's
afraid of using himself up
He goes from his little
glassed in bell
jar office into a
hermetically sealed room where
he wraps himself in stillness
takes out his cock
He thinks he can squeeze
everything into

where he wants it like
books in the Dewey
Decimal system. He thinks if
he moves the is from
penis it will
turn into a pen

He orders his nights like a
file, bloodless as his
library. The only warm living
thing he has are
his cats. And sometimes
he drugs them

Now his tools are all
spread out neatly
assembled but never
used. He tries to get
started takes the
phone off the hook like
someone about to make
love squeezes and pushes
tries to conjure up some
giant sheet white

and cool and soothing
giving like the skin in

side a thigh waiting for
something from him to make a
mark. He even strokes him
self with a feather. He never
thought it would be so
hard to make some
thing out of nothing

make something move him,
moves his penis toward the
feather pours another
glass of wine puts
on a different record.
The stillness castrates him.

His pen is
like a penis made
of fluff he twists and
sweats rubs his head
between his hands

Whatever was hard and
strong has gone into cutting
up women. This is not the
first time nothing
comes its like the night
he tried to stuff

himself inside me as if
some of my words would ooze
thru the tip of where
he should have been
more sensitive and he
couldn't get it in

stuffed himself there like
soggy kleenex. Tried
each of my holes then kicked
me out with the books
nobody used much
saying he was a romantic

and suddenly sees how it all
is dry as leaves
sees the eraser
as a nipple screams
slams the typewriter but all
that comes is a little

blood some broken keys
and bruises that look
like what they
aren't too

FRIDAY APRIL 8

The wind is ever grayer
snow at the foot of the bed
I dream ice claws in the pillows
The man who deals in stained glass
comes in a 3 piece blue tweed suit
wax on his mustache
handlebars of hair
but it's hard to imagine riding it
I'm in bone and navy blue
subdued as those colors
He laughs when I say McDonald's is fine
puts his arm around a little tight
for a talk on stained glass
pulls me out in the too clean BMW
into a restaurant
full of other men in 3 piece suits

shoes you could see their
balls in except for the wool legs
when we drink chablis
I feel the navy turn lighter
more royal than sky
We don't leave till it's almost 5
talking about a little
place we'd both like in the
Berkshires and the look of light at
4 o clock The wind makes a
lot of things look like
what they aren't

ATLANTIC CITY

I wear a tight
Hiawatha looking
dress as tight as
a hookers stagger
in 6 inch tall
skinny spikes
heels that catch
in the boardwalk
in the salt night
my hair frizzy
The sailors rub
their eyes from
my maybelline cats
eyes to my
slick tanned
legs, my mother
2 steps behind

IT MUST HAVE BEEN SEXY

sister in the seventh
or the peonies color of
untanned skin and a rosy
crotch that made the man
with a mustache pull
my skirt away from
my body saying he
would if he could
as he asked if I'd
like to play and cupped
my ass like it was a
melon he'd already
bought and could use
any way he wanted
in the privacy of it
must have been sleek
hair of the Black
Eclipse reminding him
of other slippery
shiny black places
Slippery was what he
was, with his name as
elusive as the ring that
was there and then
wasn't. He asked if I
was legal if I'd like
to swim in the lake
of his body, tho of
course he didn't say it
like I did right here
His lips and fingers
seemed to feel assured
of immunity it was as
if I was one of many
gloves the pair most

handy and he was hot,
out for a big heist
that there'd be no
traces of in the
morning

ARACHNE LIANE

very good with her
fingers and also
with her tongue
lips glistening a
legend everyone wanted
to watch her
she almost opened a
studio to teach what could
grow from her mouth
boasted she could spin
any man into her
make him do what
others couldn't
make and keep him
hard as zinc her
spells, webs you find
on the grass before
it rains Spanish moss
extravagantly beautiful
and deadly

PENTHOUSE PLAYBOY

no women wear under
wear show their
beautiful bush thru
a hole in the kitchen
floor to workmen in
the cellar who've

come to fix a crack
and of course do
Nobody ever has a
period or hair
where it shouldn't
be. Cocks are always
9 inches and throb
bing and women's
tits point to the
sky they never
have to worry a
bout lawbriefs or
poems or food but
hang out at rallies
drug stores and
on planes in their
blonde hair like
vampires under
a full moon that
starved for hot
blood they rip
zippers bulging
jeans and the mounds
under wool open with
their white teeth
it doesn't matter
if there's a druggist
or people buying
dramamine or voting
democratic even
in a crowded elevator
between floors these
women dive through
leather with their
own crotch hairs
always dripping
like a porpoise

WRITING ABOUT DEATH

at Syracuse in
a cashmere skirt I
went to your apartment
intrigued by your cane
but I wore a panty girdle

dreams you said in the
tiny living room dreams
were what mattered,
pulled me toward the
bedroom to see what
you'd written under
the floor

when I wouldn't you
snarled and gave me
orange juice and
said we all get old
and if nothing happens

come back and lie near
me in bed. I never
did. Once when we
were fighting my
ex husband dragged
home a book,
as proud of discovering
you as he was of
meditation weights
and bringing back
patrick sky

When I laughed he
threw the book
in the garage

I still have your Denial of
but I haven't opened
it it's strange you
had no idea you
were dying when you
wrote it strange
what I denied you I'd
have so much trouble
getting rid of

WEEDS AND WOODSMOKE

your tattoo that
one gold earring

how your red beard
was only red in
places Love,
your strong tongue

pieces of a night
coming back like
petals in the only
kind of flower
i can draw

wild, bright
not connected
to any center

IT'S LIKE A WOMAN

who tells you such
intimate details
fast she makes
a wall around her
not a window

things seem
a certain way

listen we'll write
each other or
we won't just

don't look
close don't
call it a

thing relation
ship we're each
in our own boat
in the night

dots on a
Seurat painting
that seem to but
really don't touch

SMOTHER MOTHER

the mother who wasn't
a daughter gladly who has
always felt she should have
been a son needs to
be needed may by page 17
smother mother her child But

say a daughter tries to lug
another (unapproved) body
close and its:
you thanked him so much
when he brought in the rabbit
but you didn't honey thank

me for the tea you're
so masochistic lyn I think
I'll try being a masochist no
sadistic to you honey you

can take me to dinner I
know the way you pay for him
and the chocolate wasn't
that good even if I was a
mean mother I'd wish you

a daughter like you are
so you would know

Someday you'll regret the
time you didn't spend with
me tho I don't want you
to regret anything

Honey your orange tree died
because you're not good to yourself

THAT YEAR THEY MOVED IN

to the flat on the hill
something dark was moving
toward Europe my father
worked in his rich brother's
store and stopped reading
or saying much it was
so gradual my mother
didn't say a thing sat
on her side of the black
Plymouth thinking maybe
of the men she didn't
wouldn't thinking never
Rumours of war burned thru

their sleep were in the
park where you could
say something and the whisper
went to other people's
houses. Everyone wore grey.
Buildings a whole
town the color of granite
and the dim light in the
Brown Derby where they went
to drink beer that whole
spring waiting for me as
bright as warm as they'd
be for a while

RIDING UPSTATE SHE TELLS ME

about the night with
gramp and the Polish
girl on either side
of the bed where
she was sleeping
downstairs in the den
not up in the worst of
the upstairs bedrooms
being the only
girl and the first
a disappointment
that room so small
there couldn't
be any mirror no
heat but this one
night with the
flu feeling the
hired girl and her
father giggling
whispering pushing
toward each other

no lights on but
what came thru
apple branches my
mother pretending
to be asleep smell
of Blue Danube
pussy pussy and
the girl wriggling
I knew she said some
thing wasn't right

LIKE WITH MY EX

inlaws, pretending
and smiling lapping
up the table
lapping up crumbs
becoming a lint
detector not touching
that cat not
touching myself
hiding my hair
hiding my feelings
playing the role
you wanted not saying
I was hungry or
wasn't or didn't
want to be touched
agreeing to such
playing and sucking
up to then missing the
new leaves because
my head was down in
his lap like a
napkin for him
able to spit this
anger out just

on paper as
if what I really
felt would cause
such whiplash
no one could
go on

FAMILY

she said horses they
lived somewhere with
black horses in the
snow that the fruit
was so huge in Odessa
and a father or was
it a cousin marrying
late and not the girl
who was dancing in
the candles the night
before they were
to marry her dress
eating fire as May
wind blew in from
the black trees
and left her ash

PHOTOGRAPHS OF MOTHERS AND DAUGHTERS

you can almost always
see the mother's hands

the daughter usually
nests in a curve of
the mother's hair or
neck like it was a cave

the way cats do the
night it starts to snow.

some seem to suck
on the mother's breath
you might think the
mother had eyes
in her fingers

often her hands
are on the daughters
shoulders pulling
her close as if

she wanted to press
her back inside

MOTHER AND DAUGHTER PHOTOS

my mother and my sister
near an old black sixties
Chevy my sister in a
nest between my mother's
arms you can just see
certain parts of my mother
like a branch in a back
drop I'm in several with
her standing in back her
arms around me her prize
melon a book just she
would write. I remember
the rabbi said enjoy
your wedding after that
it will be your husband
and your child I've
noticed this in several
other photos of mothers

with their girls the
daughter held up close in
front like someone with
a desperate sign words
pointing west or saying
Hartford the daughter
almost blots the mother
out it's as if there
was some huge dark hole
only a camera would pick
up where something that
had got away had been

WE ARE TALKING ABOUT THINGS I DON'T REMEMBER: OR, ON THE FAULT LINE

to smooth over the holes
we've punched fighting,
a few pebbles for the
story of my father coming
home each night picking me
up in the air reading
three little piggies

Smooth them down with
how I said at my sister's
blue eyes oh Mama everyone
will think it's odd your
eyes are brown and mine
and Ben's. The ruts are

still there but it's a little
less rocky with the story
of the man I hugged upstairs
remember the black salve
Remember the strawberries

When the cellar floods I
stay an extra day and fall
asleep in the backseat
driving till one to look
for a place to dry the rags.
I'm her 107lb baby. But
by morning I have to go
and there's little quakes

the house is suddenly on
some dangerous fault
shaking I run back in
to check for keys she's
forgotten something and
follows puts her hand
out to make a lap for me
to sit on count to

ten she says and then
she does it as we would
each time we ran up the
double flight of the
apartment to check for
burning cigarettes,
something wrong

MY MOTHER SAYING NO I

didn't do it when I
punched the boy next door
in the sand my daughter

is beautiful and smart
she wouldn't jump in an
open grave she told

the Girl Scout leader
she wouldn't kick Mr.
Dewey in the back

seat of the car all
the way to Montpelier
My daughter isn't really

fat my daughter does
science projects of
the eye tho she doesn't

see right she isn't
asked to dance because
she's smart my daughter

looks good in whatever
she puts on take out
the dirty words and

you'd love her poems
my daughter if she'd
just pull the hair

from her eyes not waste
herself on the wrong
it must be something
that I've done my
daughter in the rain
with her hair curling

if I rub her back
maybe she'll sleep
She can do anything

who wouldn't want
I just wish I could
make her know

CAPE COD

somewhere in a raised
ranch my husband
waiting for the
phone in rooms he
left when it was
snowing now he
expects everything
to be as it was
In Italy the new
man keeps sending
postcards my sister
wishes she had my
body to hold the man
in the air who feeds
her turtles in that
small yellow room
Vermont dissolves
We drove too long

it's late my mother
puts lysol in the
tub complains about
the cottage I step
on the scale naked
with the door locked
The way the numbers
rush past 100 could
be the years ahead

HAIR

in college i wore
it up was accused of
someone taking my
test for me

relatives were always
smoothing it down putting
pins in it as if it
was some strange night
beast animal dark
weeds to cut back

when I was six in the
cottage I'd comb it
straight in the wet
sun but it didn't
stay it was like

fat like my fat
thighs that looked
thin in the late
afternoon shadows

they had their fat
way in the mirror
in the damp room

tho i wanted to be
skinny with long
straight hair
dieted till i

passed out put
curlfree on my hair
and just got it
orange as plastic
as a broom

in the 70's
people in airports
would laugh would
snear hippie i

tucked it up in
to itself for in
laws bosses

english examining
men and superintendents
knotted it tight
like a hair ball
inside a cat
a pearl waiting
nests for some
thing inside i

hated not being able
to let it down hated
twisting it twisting
myself into what was
neat, small expected

i was sorry i wasn't
indian wished that
it would grow long
enough to hold out
buildings as if i
could climb out into
my new self that way

WHEN I'M AROUND CARL I DON'T

eat otherwise she says
I've been stuffing
myself pigged
out on my birth
day see the cow
boy boots my
father gave me
and my mother's

skis sweaters
you get more
when they're
trying to out
do each other
when my father
lived home it
wasn't this way
a new suede coat
Jordache jeans
pigged out didn't
dream kept eating
pizza got a pearl
brooch earrings
2 cakes I ate
frosting off
of even that
day tho my dad
bitched at having
to pick me up

MY FATHER STARTED TO

die eating donuts
the salt wind on
the pier Old Orchard
photographs of
movie stars 6 for
a quarter Vera Lynn
Merle I remember
there wasn't any
sound we got in
the car fast left
the motel and drove
to Malden His
sister made calls

in a quiet voice and
my sister and I
examined our rubber
dolls their skin
turned brown by
sun in the car's
back seat window
we didn't know
how quiet we had
to be in the house
that smelled so
Jewish we hadn't
thought we'd go
back there after
the time that Sophie
piled chicken
liver on my father's
plate scolded us
for calling him
ben having a
Christmas tree and
no star of David
we didn't know how long
we'd have to stay
with tv shows about
murder we couldn't
shut out in the
cold dark room

LOVE LIKE SHOPLIFTING

A challenge,
silver dollars on
the railroad track
with the train
coming, flashing
light up in

the leaves. Love,
you could be
the jack of hearts,
something I don't
need, probably
won't use but
start, like dropping
the priceless sword
into stretched out
nylon bikinis and
walking to the
door as if metal
wasn't rubbing
the lips under that
hair. A game, six
pair of velvet pants
crushed into
boots under my
skin tight straight
skirt slit to
my knees that I'm
walking casually in as if
there were years to
get past the door
before zippers burst like
spit balls grenades
and what's inside slams out
like fat or tears
giving what's
what away

IT STARTS OFF SMALL AS A KITTEN YOU CAN
CARRY AROUND IN YOUR PALM

kept off the bed
you think you can hide
it tell it where

to go you never
dream it could change your habits

suddenly it's digging
scratching your heart
in the middle of the
night you hardly
have anybody over

it's like that old
woman who took the
heiffer born the
day her last son
died into her bed
room wrapped it

in an old flannel
robe she said it
grew so fast four
years but it seems
days and now I can't
get it out the door

RAMONA LAKE

in the back row of a
class that wouldn't listen
with her 70 IQ and
enormous pleading eyes

saucers of licorice
"I want to learn"
over the loud chain
saw buzz of boys
laughing guffawing

"I'd like to pass the
bar too." Ramona
in your pink check
dress hair so black
it was close to blue

still as a mannequin
oblivious to spit
balls pokes in the
ribs Ramona I
couldn't teach you

old enough now to have
a daughter as startled
paralyzed as the one
deer frozen
in car lights

baffled suddenly
in another world

MY MOTHER WAS WATCHING

tv on the sofa with
the spot from where
she threw chlorox
when the grey cat
peed when he called
She said no she
wouldn't meet him
she was falling a
sleep in the huge
living room that
should be painted
got up maybe with
snow on the tube
the wind rattling

the windows no one
had fixed for years
Only a few cars
skidding on Main St
rain that froze
that would glisten
tomorrow in the
sun be the last
thing he touches
climbing the hill
to see his lawyer
everything in his
chest flickering
like the lights
strung across the
park for Christmas

1918

a family of gypsies
comes into the store
my mother and peg
are playing in the
back of the place
in a house of shoe
boxes my grand
father dark as a
gypsy and as sly
is naturally quite
suspicious tells
the clerks to button
their eyes my mother
is dreaming of fires
and tambourines
red skirts swirling
the old woman looks
at a shoe 4 people

are watching my grand
mother comes from
behind the handbags
and corsets the
old gypsy shrugs no
everyone breathes
easy as they go but
she comes back in
15 minutes with the
shoes like a cat
with a rabbit and
she says you were
all watching me so
I had to prove I
could now they're
yours

RINK

going to town with
out my mother going
to town with the
hired girl as the
G.I.'s in trenches
were listening to
rumors going home
in part of their
head and my hair
was curly my thighs
fat in a bathing
suit for someone
older the noise
at the rink blurs
and louis armstrong
comes over lake
champlain i forget
those stories of

what happened in
german tunnels
here it was light
and i could do it
a girl with one
blue eye and the
other green twirled
in a short skirt
that showed her
panties her perfect
thighs

LIVING ROOM

jack and jill had
drawings of fathers
in army clothes
my mother sprayed
around the new flat
turning the radio
up when somebody said
the germans it was
some time before i
realized tunnels
weren't made just for
them a sailor came
and slept with his
eyes open on the blue
couch where the cat
peed i couldn't
understand why my
grandmother kept
crying forgot the
ferns we peeled
the foil from gum
wrappers rolled them
into silver balls

that glowed in the
scooped out glass
elephant behind the
chair as the lights
went out bright
eggs from some odd
dangerous bird that
buzzed the houses
Sirens a blood red
arrow on the radio
the only light

MY SISTER SAYS SHE WANTS ME TO COME AND READ THRU THIRTY YEARS OF DIARIES

in the house overlooking
rain bent pines,
in the life others
would envy she looses her
self in fragments how
could we have changed so
she asks over the
phone how could I not
still be eleven in front
of the old Plymouth
on Main Street,
Mother younger there
than I am now. Beginnings.
What might go, pressed
flat as a daisy from
Porter Field from
someone she tries to
remember like a deaf
man remembering an
opera he heard
eleven years before
My sister fragile as

113

in demand as those flowers
has found her days
losing color turning thin as
breakable as those near
transparent brittle
leaves. Nothing bends
like the pines her
days are a shelf of
blown glass buds
a heart beat
could shatter. Come
she says we can laugh
at what seemed so
serious then maybe from
what happened in the
apartment when the
roof fell in or
at Nanny's as Herbert
was dying we can
know something about
the stories we
haven't begun yet

WRITING CLASS SYRACUSE WINTER

write he said looking
like an even craggier
Lincoln your impressions
the next 4 days details
of a walk across campus.
Even now I remember I
wore a strawberry wool
skirt, matching sweater.
There was bittersweet
near the Hall of Language.
I curled in a window
ledge of a cave in Crouse,

an organ drifting thru
smooth warm wood. I
could let the wine
dark light hold me, slid
on the ice behind where a
man with a blue mole
picked me up, my notes
scattering up Comstock.
Torn tights, knees snow
kissed the skin off. I
was hypnotised by that
huge growth said yes
tho I only half remembered.
Upstairs icicles clotted,
wrapped glass in gauze.
There must have been some
one who didn't call. Blue
walls ugly green bedspread.
Dorothy popping gum eating
half a tuna sandwich before
we'd lie in bed with the
lights out wondering what
it would be like to have
Dr. Fox with his red beard
go down on us as we

braided and rubbed our
mahogany hair dry and I
tried to figure out what to
do with the bittersweet,
torn knees, ragged maples,
didn't believe I'd ever
have anything to write about

NOVEMBER 1 BOOGIE

on the third floor
rug rolled back
shoes under the sofa
toes instead of words
hair swinging like
Spanish moss in
to a slow blues
kelp tangling in
water that shakes
hips and lips free
skin making love to
a whole room no
wonder the Shakers
danced till they
couldn't stand
went home with
grass stains,
starved

THE KNIFE THROWER'S WOMAN

I think of other things.
Once I itched so in the
middle of a throw but
I thought of words from
something in an old hymn.
I know the shape his
fingers take when
the steel slips thru
them think of them
outside my clothes and
then unbuttoning and
stroking and sliding. We
never talk about be
ing afraid. His

sweat isn't from any
heat. I step away
from the knife handles
like a snake shedding
its skin. It's not
me he sees. I am
the space, his snow
angel shadow in the snow
where something has been

IN A NOTEBOOK FROM PARIS

scraps the handwriting
that had sloped in the
yellow light of Florence
toward where each line
was heading, now almost
too real with its "this
is impossible" under a
line from the man sing
ing near Rue de l'Harpe
moaning where do I go
from here. I said I
didn't know how to
change anything. How
little I knew. And then
the spit out leaning
backward like trees
squashed toward the
left by monsoon winds
"I feel dead, dead,"
darkly underlined

KNEELING IN ICED BLUE GRASS 1982
THANKSGIVING

when bare branches
tapped the green
house like long
fingers and the
dog leaned and
pulled the fence
a little east as
if she could pull
3/4s of the back
yard through the
river, yelping.
Silver light
through pewter.
Leaning in iced
grass in thick wool,
pulling Brussels
sprouts from cold
blue leaves, yanked
the small green
balls, jade, cold
marbles at the
top of the stalk
like jewels on
the sleet glazed
branches, holding
on, bending midnights
like certain lips
on the pillow,
sweeter for
weathering some
killing frost.

BLACK HOLES AND THE MLA

it was all tweed near the elevator tweed and a crush of
beards and English accents from Dakota, Florida and
north I knew that I shouldn't have worn my black sweater
with holes musk that smelled of darkest midnight. It must
have been my nighttime smell that pulled the red faced
man off the elevator sniffing toward where I sat like
someone waiting to see a professor who gave them a
failing grade. He sniffed right up to the black said he was
big in Wallace Stevens and had anybody asked me out yet
to eat. Black was all wrong for the MLA I knew especially
black velvet. I shouldn't have written such frank poems
before I came I wrote to my sister making the four foot
tall Chaucer man suppose I'd swoon when he spit out
cock cunt and fuck and ask me to want him. He had
black spots on his hand black shiny shoes and asked if I
slept with a black man. He said he was hurt when I called
him Dr. Couldn't I call him Ted. He wanted me on his lap
with my dress up and my crotch soaking tho I said I lived
like a nun. Maybe this is why nuns gave up black dresses I
thought as he pulled my hand toward where forty years
earlier there might have been something to touch. It must
have been the black that made him think I'd care for what
he had upstairs pant while he was talking about his
academic connections. If I just could have worn my pussy
on my chin and shoplifted a tweed jacket It was the black
holes they wanted to jump in as if I was a planet that had
collapsed into itself a huge black hole of surprises